Emily's House

Emily's House

BY *Niko Scharer*

PICTURES BY *Joanne Fitzgerald*

A Groundwood Book

Douglas & McIntyre
Toronto / Vancouver

Canadian Cataloguing in Publication Data

Scharer, Niko, 1965-
    Emily's house

ISBN 0-88899-111-8

I. Fitzgerald, Joanne, 1956-   . II. Title.

PS8587.C493E5 1990   jC813'.54   C90-093593-6
PZ7.S36Em 1990

A Groundwood Book
Douglas & McIntyre Ltd.
585 Bloor Street West
Toronto, Ontario M6G 1K5

Design by Michael Solomon
Printed and bound in Hong Kong
by Everbest Printing Co. Ltd.

For Meg

N.S.

For my family and friends

J.F.

Emily lived in a little brick house
With a creaky old door and a little brown mouse.
Emily listened, and Emily frowned
'Cause Emily heard two very loud sounds!
For the door went creak
And the mouse went squeak
And Emily cried with a great big tear
And she said, "There's too much noise in here!"

Well, Emily sighed, "Oh what to do?"
But the mouse said, "Get us a pussycat too."

So Emily left in her white straw hat
And she came back home with a tabby cat.
And the door went creak
And the mouse went squeak
And the cat meow-ed
And meow-ed so loud
That Emily cried with a great big tear
And she said, "There's too much noise in here!"

Well, Emily sighed, "Oh what to do?"
But the mouse said, "Get us a puppy dog too."

So Emily left with a jig and a jog
And she came back home with a puppy dog.
And the door went creak
And the mouse went squeak
And the cat meow-ed
And the dog bow-wow-ed
And Emily cried with a great big tear
And she said, "There's too much noise in here!"

Well, Emily sighed, "Oh what to do?"
But the mouse said, "Get us a black sheep too."

Marilea McAllister

So Emily left with a bounding leap
And she came back home with a small black sheep.
And the door went creak
And the mouse went squeak
And the cat meow-ed
And the dog bow-wow-ed
And the sheep went baa
I want my maa
And Emily cried with a great big tear
And she said, "There's too much noise in here!"

Well, Emily sighed, "Oh what to do?"
But the mouse said, "Get us a billy goat too."

So Emily left with a five pound note
And she came back home with a billy goat.
And the door went creak
And the mouse went squeak
And the cat meow-ed
And the dog bow-wow-ed
And the sheep went baa
And the goat went maa
And Emily cried with a great big tear
And she said, "There's too much noise in here!"

Well, Emily sighed, "Oh what to do?"
But the mouse said, "We need a brown cow too."

So Emily left, and I don't know how,
But she came back home with a big brown cow.
And the door went creak
And the mouse went squeak
And the cat meow-ed
And the dog bow-wow-ed
And the sheep went baa
And the goat went maa
And the cow went moo
And the noise just grew
And Emily cried with a great big tear
And she said, "There's too much noise in here!"

Well, Emily sighed, "Oh what to do?"
But the mouse said, "Get me a turtle dove too."

So Emily left with a push and a shove
And she came back home with a turtle dove.
And the door went creak
And the mouse went squeak
And the cat meow-ed
And the dog bow-wow-ed
And the sheep went baa
And the goat went maa
And the cow went moo
And the dove went coo
And Emily cried with a great big tear
And she yelled,
"THERE'S TOO MUCH NOISE IN HERE!"

Well, Emily didn't know what to do
But the mouse said, "Just try one thing new."

And he sent the cat and the dog and more
Why he sent all the animals out of the door.
And the door went creak
And the mouse went squeak
And Emily listened, and Emily smiled!
And she sighed the sigh of a happy child.

'Cause all she heard in her little brick house
Was a small sort of creak and the squeak of a mouse.